Hand in Hand

Hand in Hand

AN AMERICAN HISTORY THROUGH POETRY

COLLECTED BY LEE BENNETT HOPKINS

ILLUSTRATED BY PETER M. FIORE

SIMON & SCHUSTER
BOOKS FOR YOUNG READERS

PUBLISHED BY SIMON & SCHUSTER

NEW YORK LONDON TORONTO SYDNEY TOKYO SINGAPORE

SIMON & SCHUSTER
BOOKS FOR YOUNG READERS
1230 Avenue of the Americas, New York, New York 10020

SIMON & SCHUSTER BOOKS FOR YOUNG READERS
is a trademark of Simon & Schuster.

Book design by Sylvia Frezzolini
The text for this book is set in Garamond.
The illustrations are oil paintings.

Manufactured in the United States of America

10 9 8 7 6 5 4 3 2 1

Library of Congress Cataloging-in-Publication Data
Hand in hand : An American history through poetry /
[compiled] by Lee Bennett Hopkins;
illustrated by Peter M.Fiore.   p. cm. Includes indexes.
Summary: A collection of poems and lyrics from several
songs provides a look at our country, from colonial times
to the present.
1. United States—Juvenile poetry. 2. Children's poetry, American.
[1. United States—Poetry. 2. American poetry—Collections.]
I. Hopkins, Lee Bennett. II. Fiore, Peter M., ill.
PS595.U5M9 1993 811.914080282—dc20   92-24230 CIP
ISBN: 0-671-73315-X

CONTENTS

Contents

INTRODUCTION

Poets have always been fascinated with America and its many facets—its history, its land, its people, its promise, its dreams. *Hand in Hand* is a sweeping history of the United States through poetry, organized by eras and themes that mark our country's beginnings and expansion from the early 1600s to the 21st century.

This poetic panorama rings out with strong voices of great past masters, such as Henry Wadsworth Longfellow, Carl Sandburg, and Langston Hughes. Thoughts of contemporary poets, such as Lucille Clifton, Cynthia Rylant, and Paul Janeczko, also resound throughout the volume, as do new voices, including Lillian M. Fisher, Isabel Joshlin Glaser, and Beverly McLoughland, showcased here for the first time.

Since poetry is uniquely qualified to transcend the span of time, the order of the selections is based on the subject matter rather than the chronology of when the poems were actually written. Poems written long ago intermingle with modern poems that reflect on the same milestones of our rich history. Words by poets such as Walt Whitman, written over a century ago, have as much impact on our lives today, and for all tomorrows, as when they were originally penned, emphasizing the impact poetry had, has, and continues to have.

Lee Bennett Hopkins
SCARBOROUGH, NEW YORK

ONE

COME, YE THANKFUL
PEOPLE, COME

1600s

In 1620 the *Mayflower* brought over one
hundred Pilgrims to the New World.
Landing at Cape Cod, they met Native
Americans who taught them how to cope
in this strange new territory.

In mid-October 1621 the first
Thanksgiving was held. People raised "the
song of harvest-home."

A new world was beginning.

The Gift Outright

The land was ours before we were the land's.
She was our land more than a hundred years
Before we were her people. She was ours
In Massachusetts, in Virginia,
But we were England's, still colonials,
Possessing what we still were unpossessed by,
Possessed by what we now no more possessed.
Something we were withholding made us weak
Until we found out that it was ourselves
We were withholding from our land of living,
And forthwith found salvation in surrender.
Such as we were we gave ourselves outright
(The deed of gift was many deeds of war)
To the land vaguely realizing westward,
But still unstoried, artless, unenhanced,
Such as she was, such as she would become.

Robert Frost

The Landing of the Pilgrim Fathers

The breaking waves dashed high
　　On a stern and rock-bound coast,
And the woods, against a stormy sky,
　　Their giant branches tossed;

And the heavy night hung dark
　　The hills and waters o'er,
When a band of exiles moored their bark
　　On the wild New England shore.

Not as the conqueror comes,
　　They, the true-hearted, came:
Not with the roll of the stirring drums,
　　And the trumpet that sings of fame;

Not as the flying come,
　　In silence and in fear,—
They shook the depths of the desert's gloom
　　With their hymns of lofty cheer.

Amidst the storm they sang,
　　And the stars heard, and the sea;
And the sounding aisles of the dim woods rang
　　To the anthem of the free!

The ocean-eagle soared
　　From his nest by the white wave's foam,

And the rocking pines of the forest roared;
This was their welcome home!

There were men with hoary hair
Amidst that pilgrim-band;
Why had they come to wither there,
Away from their childhood's land?

There was woman's fearless eye,
Lit by her deep love's truth;
There was manhood's brow, serenely high,
And the fiery heart of youth.

What sought they thus afar?
Bright jewels of the mine?
The wealth of seas, the spoils of war?—
They sought a faith's pure shrine!

Aye, call it holy ground,
The soil where first they trod!
They have left unstained what there they found—
Freedom to worship God!

Felicia Dorothea Hemans

First Thanksgiving

Three days we had,
       feasting, praying, singing.

Three days outdoors at wooden tables,
Colonists and Indians together,
Celebrating a full harvest,
A golden summer of corn.

We hunted the woods, finding
Venison, deer, and wild turkey.

We brought our plump geese and ducks,
Great catches of silver fish.

We baked corn meal bread with nuts,
Journey cake, and steaming succotash.

We roasted the meat on spits
Before huge, leaping fires.

We stewed our tawny pumpkins
In buckets of bubbling maple sap.

Three days we had,
        feasting, praying, singing

Three days outdoors at wooden tables,
Colonists and Indians together,
Celebrating a full harvest,
Praying, each to our God.

Myra Cohn Livingston

Circles

The white man drew a small circle in the sand
and told the red man, "This is what the Indian
knows," and drawing a big circle around the
small one, "This is what the white man knows."
The Indian took the stick and swept an immense
ring around both circles: "This is where the
white man and the red man know nothing."

Carl Sandburg

Come, Ye Thankful People, Come

Come, ye thankful people, come,
Raise the song of harvest-home:
All is safely gathered in
Ere the winter storms begin:
God, our Maker, doth provide
For our wants to be supplied;
Come to God's own temple, come,
Raise the song of harvest-home.

George J. Elvey

Two
RING! OH, RING
FOR LIBERTY!

1700s

The American Revolution began on April 19, 1775, when British "red-coats" clashed with colonists in Lexington, Massachusetts, and nearby Concord.

Between 1775 and 1783 the war was fought between Great Britain and the thirteen original colonies of North America.

George Washington, who served as the commander in chief of the Continental Army, was inaugurated as our first president on April 30, 1789.

The war led to the birth of a new kind of nation—the United States. This new nation would "ring, oh, ring for liberty!"

GEORGIA

SOUTH CAROLINA

NORTH CAROLINA

VIRGINIA

PENNSYLVANIA

MARYLAND

DELAWARE

NEW JERSEY

NEW YORK

RHODE ISLAND

CONNECTICUT

MASSACHUSETTS

MAINE

Paul Revere's Ride

Listen, my children, and you shall hear
Of the midnight ride of Paul Revere,
On the eighteenth of April, in Seventy-five;
Hardly a man is now alive
Who remembers that famous day and year.

He said to his friend, "If the British march
By land or sea from the town to-night,
Hang a lantern aloft in the belfry arch
Of the North Church tower as a signal light,—
One, if by land, and two, if by sea;
And I on the opposite shore will be,
Ready to ride and spread the alarm
Through every Middlesex village and farm,
For the country-folk to up and to arm."

Then he said, "Good night!" and with muffled oar
Silently rowed to the Charlestown shore,
Just as the moon rose over the bay,
Where swinging wide at her moorings lay
The *Somerset*, British man-of-war;
A phantom ship, with each mast and spar
Across the moon like a prison bar,
And a huge black hulk, that was magnified
By its own reflection in the tide.

Meanwhile, his friend, through alley and street,
Wanders and watches with eager ears,
Till in the silence around him he hears
The muster of men at the barrack door,
The sound of arms, and the tramp of feet,
And the measured tread of the grenadiers,
Marching down to their boats on the shore.

Then he climbed to the tower of the Old North Church
By the wooden stairs, with stealthy tread,
To the belfry-chamber overhead,
And startled the pigeons from their perch
On the somber rafters, that round him made
Masses and moving shapes of shade,—
By the trembling ladder, steep and tall,
To the highest window in the wall,
Where he paused to listen and look down
A moment on the roofs of the town,
And the moonlight flowing over all.

Beneath in the churchyard, lay the dead,
In their night-encampment on the hill,
Wrapped in silence so deep and still
That he could hear, like a sentinel's tread,
The watchful night-wind as it went
Creeping along from tent to tent,
And seeming to whisper, "All is well!"
A moment only he feels the spell
Of the place and the hour, and the secret dread
Of the lonely belfry and the dead;

For suddenly all his thoughts are bent
On a shadowy something far away,
Where the river widens to meet the bay,—
A line of black that bends and floats
On the rising tide, like a bridge of boats.

Meanwhile, impatient to mount and ride,
Booted and spurred, with a heavy stride
On the opposite shore walked Paul Revere.
Now he patted his horse's side,
Now gazed at the landscape far and near,
Then, impetuous, stamped the earth,
And turned and tightened his saddle-girth;
But mostly he watched with eager search
The belfry-tower of the Old North Church,
As it rose above the graves on the hill,
Lonely and spectral and somber and still.
And lo! as he looks, on the belfry's height
A glimmer, and then a gleam of light!
He springs to the saddle, the bridle he turns,
But lingers and gazes, till full on his sight
A second lamp in the belfry burns!

A hurry of hoofs in a village street,
A shape in the moonlight, a bulk in the dark,
And beneath, from the pebbles, in passing, a spark
Struck out by a steed flying fearless and fleet:
That was all! And yet, through the gloom and the light,
The fate of a nation was riding that night;

And the spark struck out by that steed, in his flight,
Kindled the land into flame with its heat.

He has left the village and mounted the steep,
And beneath him, tranquil and broad and deep,
Is the Mystic, meeting the ocean tides;
And under the alders that skirt its edge,
Now soft on the sand, now loud on the ledge,
Is heard the tramp of his steed as he rides.

It was twelve by the village clock,
When he crossed the bridge into Medford town.
He heard the crowing of the cock,
And the barking of the farmer's dog,
And felt the damp of the river fog,
That rises after the sun goes down.

It was one by the village clock,
When he galloped into Lexington.
He saw the gilded weathercock
Swim in the moonlight as he passed,
And the meeting-house windows, blank and bare,
Gaze at him with a spectral glare,
As if they already stood aghast
At the bloody work they would look upon.

It was two by the village clock,
When he came to the bridge in Concord town.
He heard the beating of the flock,
And the twitter of birds among the trees,

And felt the breath of the morning breeze
Blowing over the meadows brown.
And one was safe and asleep in his bed
Who at the bridge would be first to fall,
Who that day would be lying dead,
Pierced by a British musket-ball.

You know the rest. In the books you have read,
How the British Regulars fired and fled,—
How the farmers gave them ball for ball,
From behind each fence and farmyard wall,
Chasing the red-coats down the lane,
Then crossing the fields to emerge again
Under the trees at the turn of the road,
And only pausing to fire and load.

So through the night rode Paul Revere;
And so through the night went his cry of alarm
To every Middlesex village and farm,—
A cry of defiance and not of fear,
A voice in the darkness, a knock at the door,
And a word that shall echo forevermore!
For, borne on the night-wind of the Past,
Through all our history, to the last,
In the hour of darkness and peril and need,
The people will waken and listen to hear
The hurrying hoof-beats of that steed,
And the midnight message of Paul Revere.

Henry Wadsworth Longfellow

Paul Revere Speaks

Yes,
Longfellow wrote about me.
That midnight ride in '75 to Lexington.
Adams and Hancock were old friends.
I was there at the Boston Tea Party.

Yes,
I cast bronze cannons for the army
And bullets. I manufactured gunpowder,
Commanded a garrison and artillery
During the War for Independence.

Yes,
I worked for the Constitution's ratification.
Made the first issue of paper currency,
Copper fittings for Old Ironsides, church bells,
And the state seal they still use in Massachusetts.

But
I made a good many silver pieces too.
Pitchers, bowls, coffee pots, trays.
On those I put my initials or my last name.
There are some things a man needs to be
Remembered by that only *his* hands can make.

Myra Cohn Livingston

John Hancock

"There,"
he said,
signing
his name

BIG,

BOLD,

FAT.

"King George
won't need
spectacles
to see
that!

He can read
it from here
to his
British dock,"

proclaimed
the rebellious

John Hancock.

Lee Bennett Hopkins

Ring!
Oh, Ring
for
Liberty

Molly Pitcher

All day the great guns barked and roared;
All day the big balls screeched and soared;
All day, 'mid the sweating gunners grim,
Who toiled in their smoke-shroud dense and dim,
Sweet Molly labored with courage high,
With steady hand and watchful eye,
Till the day was ours, and the sinking sun
Looked down on the field of Monmouth won,
And Molly standing beside her gun.

Now, Molly, rest your weary arm!
Safe, Molly, all is safe from harm.
Now, woman, bow your aching head,
And weep in sorrow o'er your dead!

Next day on that field so hardly won,
Stately and calm stands Washington,
And looks where our gallant Greene doth lead
A figure clad in motley weed—
A soldier's cap and a soldier's coat
Masking a woman's petticoat.
He greets our Molly in kindly wise;
He bids her raise her tearful eyes;
And now he hails her before them all
Comrade and soldier, whate'er befall,
"And since she has played a man's full part,
A man's reward for her loyal heart!

And Sergeant Molly Pitcher's name
Be writ henceforth on the shield of fame!"

Oh, Molly, with your eyes so blue!
Oh, Molly, Molly, here's to you!
Sweet honor's roll will aye be richer
To hold the name of Molly Pitcher.

Laura E. Richards

Independence Bell

JULY 4, 1776

There was a tumult in the city
In the quaint old Quaker town,
And the streets were rife with people
Pacing restless up and down—
People gathering at corners,
Where they whispered each to each,
And the sweat stood on their temples
With the earnestness of speech.

As the bleak Atlantic currents
Lashed the wild Newfoundland shore,
So they beat against the State House,
So they surged against the door;
And the mingling of their voices
Made the harmony profound,
Till the quiet street of Chestnut
Was all turbulent with sound.

"Will they do it?" "Dare they do it?"
"Who is speaking?" "What's the news?"
"What of Adams?" "What of Sherman?"
"Oh, God grant they won't refuse!"
"Make some way there!" "Let me nearer!"
"I am stifling!" "Stifle then!
When a nation's life's at hazard,
We've no time to think of men!"

So they surged against the State House,
While all solemnly inside,
Sat the Continental Congress,
Truth and reason for their guide,
O'er a simple scroll debating,
Which, though simple it might be,
Yet should shake the cliffs of England
With the thunders of the free.

Far aloft in that high steeple
Sat the bellman, old and gray,
He was weary of the tyrant
And his iron-sceptered sway;
So he sat, with one hand ready
On the clapper of the bell,
When his eye could catch the signal,
The long-expected news to tell.
See! See! The dense crowd quivers
Through all its lengthy line,
As the boy beside the portal
Hastens forth to give the sign!
With his little hands uplifted,
Breezes dallying with his hair,
Hark! with deep, clear intonation
Breaks his young voice on the air.

Hushed the people's swelling murmur,
Whilst the boy cries joyously;

"Ring!" he shouts, "Ring! Grandpapa,
Ring! oh, ring for Liberty!"
Quickly at the given signal
The old bellman lifts his hand,
Forth he sends the good news, making
Iron music through the land.

How they shouted! What rejoicing!
How the old bell shook the air,
Till the clang of freedom ruffled,
The calmly gliding Delaware!
How the bonfires and the torches
Lighted up the night's repose,
And from the flames, like fabled Phoenix,
Our glorious liberty arose!

That old State House bell is silent,
Hushed is now its clamorous tongue;
But the spirit is awakened
Still is living—ever young;
And when we greet the smiling sunlight
On the fourth of each July,
We will ne'er forget the bellman
Who, betwixt the earth and sky,
Rung out, loudly, "Independence";
Which, please God, shall never die!

Anonymous

Washington

Washington, the brave, the wise, the good,
Supreme in war, in council, and in peace,
Valiant without ambition, discreet without fear,
    Confident without presumption.

In disaster, calm; in success, moderate; in all, himself.
The hero, the patriot, the Christian.
The father of nations, the friend of mankind,
Who, when had won all, renounced all,
Then sought in the bosom of his family and of
    nature, refinement,
And in the hope of religion, immortality.

Inscription at Mount Vernon

THREE

HOME OF THE BRAVE

EARLY TO MID 1800s

In 1814 Francis Scott Key penned *The Star-spangled Banner*, which became our national anthem.

The years that followed saw a country reaching, growing, expanding. There were mountains to climb, miles of plains, waterways, and deserts to travel upon—new frontiers for pioneers to conquer.

The Westward Movement opened up endless possibilities for growth and expansion. Soon the iron rail would push its "resistless way" across the country and trains would change lives forever.

Midst the need to grow there was bloodshed between frontiersmen and the Native Americans who rightfully fought for their land—a land they possessed long before "white men" decided it was theirs.

The Star-spangled Banner

Oh, say can you see by the dawn's early light
What so proudly we hail'd at the twilight's last gleaming,
Whose broad stripes and bright stars through the perilous fight
O'er the ramparts we watch'd were so gallantly streaming?
And the rockets' red glare, the bombs bursting in air,
Gave proof through the night that our flag was still there.
Oh, say does that star-spangled banner yet wave
O'er the land of the free and the home of the brave?

On the shore dimly seen through the mists of the deep,
Where the foe's haughty host in dread silence reposes,
What is that which the breeze, o'er the towering steep,
As it fitfully blows, half conceals, half discloses?
Now it catches the gleam of the morning's first beam,
In full glory reflected now shines in the stream.
'Tis the star-spangled banner, oh, long may it wave
O'er the land of the free and the home of the brave!

And where is that band who so vauntingly swore
That the havoc of war and the battle's confusion
A home and a country should leave us no more?
Their blood has wash'd out their foul footsteps' pollution.
No refuge could save the hireling and slave
From the terror of flight or the gloom of the grave.
And the star-spangled banner in triumph doth wave
O'er the land of the free and the home of the brave.

Oh, thus be it ever when freemen shall stand
Between their lov'd home and the war's desolation!
Blest with vict'ry and peace may the heav'n-rescued land
Praise the power that hath made and preserv'd us a nation!
Then conquer we must, when our cause it is just,
And this be our motto: "In God is our Trust."
And the star-spangled banner in triumph shall wave
O'er the land of the free and the home of the brave.

Francis Scott Key

Western Wagons

They went with axe and rifle, when the trail was still to blaze,
They went with wife and children, in the prairie-schooner days,
With banjo and with frying pan—Susanna, don't you cry!
For I'm off to California to get rich out there or die!

We've broken land and cleared it, but we're tired of where we are.
They say that wild Nebraska is a better place by far.
There's gold in far Wyoming, there's black earth in Ioway,
So pack up the kids and blankets, for we're moving out today!

The cowards never started and the weak died on the road,
And all across the continent the endless campfires glowed.
We'd taken land and settled—but a traveler passed by—
And we're going West tomorrow—Lordy, never ask us why!

We're going West tomorrow, where the promises can't fail.
O'er the hills in legions, boys, and crowd the dusty trail!
We shall strive and freeze and suffer. We shall die, and tame the lands.
But we're going West tomorrow, with our fortune in our hands.

Rosemary and Stephen Vincent Benét

Battle Won Is Lost

They said, "You are no longer a lad."
   I nodded.
They said, "Enter the council lodge."
   I sat.
They said, "Our land's at stake."
   I scowled.
They said, "We are at war."
   I hated.
They said, "Prepare red war symbols."
   I painted.
They said, "Count coups."
   I scalped.
They said, "You'll see friends die."
   I cringed.
They said, "Desperate warriors fight best."
   I charged.
They said, "Some will be wounded."
   I bled.
They said, "To die is glorious."
   They lied.

Phil George

Pioneers

They settled their tent pegs here
   in the desert sands gray-deep
On the ridge of a quiet wash
   where deer and bighorn sheep
Moved in a fitful wind
   under a field of sky,
Where clouds of smoke trees smoked
   and lone coyotes cried,
Where arrowweed thickets thickened
   and ironwoods hid the trail,
And the spell of heavy silence
   was breached by Gambel's Quail.
They settled their tent pegs here—
   laid weary spirits to rest
And buried their troubles and sorrows
   in the sands of the lonesome west.

Lillian M. Fisher

Casey Jones

Come all you rounders if you want to hear
The story of a brave engineer;
Casey Jones was the hogger's name,
On a big eight-wheeler, boys, he won his fame.
Caller called Casey at half-past four,
He kissed his wife at the station door,
Mounted to the cabin with orders in his hand,
And took his farewell trip to the promised land.

Casey Jones, he mounted to the cabin,
Casey Jones, with his orders in his hand!
Casey Jones, he mounted to the cabin,
Took his farewell trip into the promised land.

Put in your water and shovel in your coal,
Put your head out the window, watch the drivers roll,
I'll run her open till she leaves the rail,
'Cause we're eight hours late with the Western Mail!
He looked at his watch and his watch was slow,
Looked at the water and the water was low,
Turned to his fireboy and then he said,
"We'll get to 'Frisco, but we'll all be dead!"

Casey Jones, he mounted to the cabin,
Casey Jones, with his orders in his hand!
Casey Jones, he mounted to the cabin,
Took his farewell trip into the promised land.

Casey pulled up old Reno Hill,
Tooted for the crossing with an awful shrill,
Snakes all knew by the engine's moans
That the hogger at the throttle was Casey Jones.
He pulled up short two miles from the place,
Number Four stared him right in the face,
Turned to his fireboy, said, "You'd better jump,
'Cause there's two locomotives that're going to bump!"

Casey Jones, be mounted to the cabin,
Casey Jones, with his orders in his hand!
Casey Jones, be mounted to the cabin,
Took his farewell trip into the promised land.

Casey said, just before he died,
"There's two more roads I'd like to ride."
Fireboy said, "What can they be?"
"The Rio Grande and the Old S.P."
Mrs. Jones sat on her bed a-sighing,
Got a telegram that Casey was dying,
Said, "Go to bed, children; hush your crying,
'Cause you've got another papa on the Salt Lake Line."

Anonymous

The Railroad Cars Are Coming

The great Pacific railway,
  For California hail!
Bring on the locomotive,
  Lay down the iron rail;
Across the rolling prairies
  By steam we're bound to go,
The railroad cars are coming, humming
  Through New Mexico.
The railroad cars are coming, humming
  Through New Mexico.

The little dogs in dog-town
  Will wag each little tail;
They'll think that something's coming
  A-riding on a rail.
The rattlesnake will show its fangs,
  The owl tu-whit, tu-who,
The railroad cars are coming, humming
  Through New Mexico.
The railroad cars are coming, humming
  Through New Mexico.

Anonymous

What's the Railroad

What's the railroad to me?
I never go to see
Where it ends.
It fills a few hollows,
And makes banks for the swallows,
It sets the sand a-blowing,
And the blackberries a-growing.

Henry David Thoreau

Child of the Sun

I am Child of sand and sun,
　　of open space and sky,
Where mesa table-tops lie bare
　　and purple buttes are high.
My blood flows back a thousand years
　　to people strong and good
Who tamed this land of little rain
　　where others never could.
We made our homes of rock and earth
　　and worked the farms below,
Carried water from the stream
　　that sometimes didn't flow.
We starved, we fought our enemies,
　　but we loved and laughed and prayed,
And even in the darkest times,
　　somehow…we stayed.
Then others came to change our lives,
　　we struggled, kept our ways.
We loved our past, our ancient ones,
　　and clung to yesterdays.
I am the child of my ancestors,
　　proud child of sand and sun.
We make our home on mesa tops
　　and my people…we are one!

Lillian M. Fisher

A Song of Joys

O the engineer's joys! to go with a locomotive!
To hear the hiss of steam, the merry shriek, the
      steam-whistle, the laughing locomotive!
To push with resistless way and speed off in the distance.

Walt Whitman

John Henry

When John Henry was a little boy,
Sitting upon his father's knee,
His father said, "Look here, my boy,
You must be a steel driving man like me.
You must be a steel driving man like me."

John Henry went up on the mountain,
Just to drive himself some steel.
The rocks was so tall and John Henry so small,
He said, "Lay down hammer and squeal,"
He said, "Lay down hammer and squeal."

John Henry had a little wife,
And the dress she wore was red;
The last thing before he died,

He said, "Be true to me when I'm dead,
Oh, be true to me when I'm dead."

John Henry's wife ask him for fifteen cents,
And he said he didn't have but a dime,
Said, "If you wait till the rising sun goes down,
I'll borrow it from the man in the mine,
I'll borrow it from the man in the mine."

John Henry started on the right-hand side,
And the steam drill started on the left.
He said, "Before I'd let that steam drill beat me down,
I'd hammer my fool self to death,
Oh, I'd hammer my fool self to death."

The steam drill started at half-past six,
John Henry started the same time.
John Henry struck bottom at half-past eight,
And the steam drill didn't bottom till nine,
And the steam drill didn't bottom till nine.
John Henry said to his captain,
"A man, he ain't nothing but a man.
Before I'd let that steam drill beat me down,
I'd die with a hammer in my hand,
Oh, I'd die with a hammer in my hand."

John Henry said to his shaker,
"Shaker, why don't you sing just a few more rounds?
And before the setting sun goes down,

You're gonna hear this hammer of mine sound,
You're gonna hear this hammer of mine sound."

John Henry hammered on the mountain,
He hammered till half-past three,
He said, "This big Bend Tunnel on the C.&O. road
Is going to be the death of me,
Lord! is going to be the death of me."

John Henry had a little baby boy,
You could hold him in the palm of your hand.
The last words before he died,
"Son, you must be a steel driving man,
Son, you must be a steel driving man."
John Henry had a little woman,
And the dress she wore was red,
She went down the railroad track and never came back,
Said she was going where John Henry fell dead,
Said she was going where John Henry fell dead.

John Henry hammering on the mountain,
As the whistle blew for half-past two,
The last word I heard him say,
"Captain, I've hammered my insides in two
Lord, I've hammered my insides in two."

Anonymous

The Erie Canal

I've got a mule, her name is Sal,
Fifteen years on the Erie Canal.
She's a good old worker and a good old pal,
Fifteen years on the Erie Canal.
We've hauled some barges in our day,
Filled with lumber, coal, and hay.
And every inch of the way I know
From Albany to Buffalo.

Low bridge, everybody down!
Low bridge, for we're comin' to a town!
You can always tell your neighbor, can always tell your pal,
If you've ever navigated on the Erie Canal.

We'd better look for a job, old gal,
Fifteen years on the Erie Canal.
You bet your life I wouldn't part with Sal,
Fifteen years on the Erie Canal.
Giddap there, Sal, we've passed that lock,
We'll make Rome 'fore six o'clock,
So one more trip and then we'll go
Right straight back to Buffalo.

Low bridge, everybody down!
Low bridge, for we're comin' to a town!
You can always tell your neighbor, can always tell your pal,
If you've ever navigated on the Erie Canal.

Where would I be if I lost my pal?
Fifteen years on the Erie Canal.
Oh, I'd like to see a mule as good as Sal,
Fifteen years on the Erie Canal.
A friend of mine once got her sore,
Now he's got a broken jaw,
'Cause she let fly with her iron toe
And kicked him into Buffalo.

Low bridge, everybody down!
Low bridge, for we're comin' to a town!
You can always tell your neighbor, can always tell your pal,
If you've ever navigated on the Erie Canal.

Anonymous

*Home
of the
Brave*

$\mathcal{F}$OUR

MARCHING ON

LATE 1800s

In the North it was called the Civil War—in the South, the War Between the States.

The 1861–1865 conflict became the most important event in the history of the United States. More than fifty major battles took place on American soil: The number of soldiers who died totaled more than all Americans who perished in the American Revolution, the War of 1812, the Mexican War, the Spanish American War, World Wars I and II, and the Korean, Vietnam, and Gulf wars combined.

Few families of any race, rich or poor, were left unscathed.

Great Americans emerged from these devastating times, putting their mark on history forever.

Despite the devastation "this nation, under God" did indeed see a new birth of freedom.

Come Up from the Fields Father

Come up from the fields father, here's a letter from our
    Pete,
And come up to the front door mother, here's a letter from thy
    dear son.

Lo, tis autumn,
Lo, where the trees, deeper green, yellower and redder,
Cool and sweeten Ohio's villages with leaves fluttering in
    the moderate wind,
Where apples ripe in the orchard hang and grapes on the
    trellis'd vines,
(Smell you the smell of the grapes on the vines?
Smell you the buckwheat where the bees were lately
    buzzing?)

Above all, lo, the sky so calm, so transparent after the rain,
    and with wondrous clouds,
Below too, all calm, all vital and beautiful, and the farm
    prospers well.

Down in the fields all prospers well,
But now from the fields come father, comes at the daughter's
    call,
And come to the entry mother, to the front door come right
    away.

Marching
On

57

Fast as she can she hurries, something ominous, her steps
    trembling,
She does not tarry to smooth her hair nor adjust her cap.

Open the envelope quickly,
O this is not our son's writing, yet his name is sign'd,
O a strange hand writes for our dear son, O stricken
    mother's soul!
All swims before her eyes, flashes with black, she catches the
    main words only,
Sentences broken, *gunshot wound in the breast, cavalry
    skirmish, taken to hospital,*
At present low, but will soon be better.

Ah now the single figure to me,
Amid all teeming and wealthy Ohio with all its cities and
    farms,
Sickly white in the face and dull in the head, very faint,
By the jamb of a door leans.

Grieve not so, dear mother, (the just-grown daughter speaks
    through her sobs,
The little sisters huddle around speechless and dismay'd,)
See, dearest mother, the letter says Pete will soon be better.

Alas poor boy, he will never be better, (nor may-be needs
    to be better, that brave and simple soul,)
While they stand at home at the door he is dead already,
The only son is dead.

*Hand
in
Hand*

But the mother needs to be better,
She with thin form presently drest in black,
By day her meals untouch'd, then at night fitfully sleeping,
    often waking,
In the midnight waking, weeping, longing with one deep
    longing,
O that she might withdraw unnoticed, silent from life escape
    and withdraw,
To follow, to seek, to be with her dear dead son.

Walt Whitman

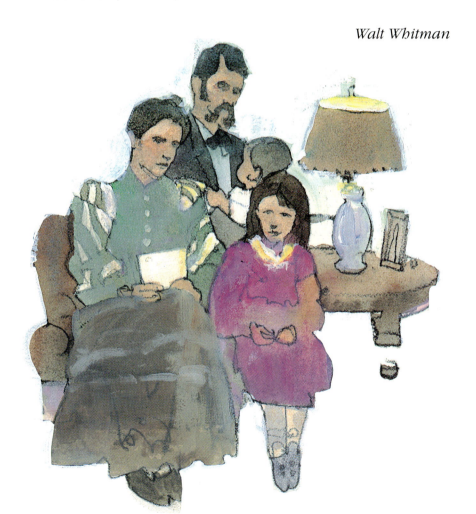

The Whippoorwill Calls

No one hears her
Coming
Through the woods
At night
For she is like
A whippoorwill
Moving through the trees
On silent wings.

No one sees her
Hiding
In the woods
By day
For she is like
A whippoorwill
Blending into leaves
On the forest floor.

And one night
The whippoorwill calls
And the warm air
Carries the haunting sound
Across the fields
And into the small dark cabins.

And only the slaves know
It is Harriet.

Beverly McLoughland

Harriet Tubman

In memory of Harriet Tubman.
Born a slave in Maryland about 1821.
Died in Auburn, New York. March 10th, 1913.
Called the Moses of her people
During the Civil War. With rare
Courage she led over three hundred
Negroes up from slavery to freedom,
And rendered invaluable service
As nurse and spy.
With implicit trust in God
She braved every danger and
Overcame every obstacle. Withal
She possessed extraordinary
Foresight and judgment so that
She truthfully said
"On my Underground Railroad
I nebber run my train off de track
An' I nebber los' a passenger."

On a tablet in Auburn, New York

John Brown's Body

John Brown's body lies a-mouldering in the grave,
John Brown's body lies slumbering in the grave—
But John Brown's soul is marching with the brave,
    His soul is marching on.

   Glory, glory, hallelujah!
   Glory, glory, hallelujah!
   Glory, glory, hallelujah!
     His soul is marching on.

He has gone to be a soldier in the Army of the Lord;
He is sworn as a private in the ranks of the Lord,—
He shall stand at Armageddon with his brave old sword,
    When Heaven is marching on.

He shall file in front where the lines of battle form,
He shall face to front when the squares of battle form—
Time with the column, and charge in the storm,
    When men are marching on.

Ah, foul Tyrants! do ye hear him where he comes?
Ah, black traitor! do ye know him as he comes,
In thunder of the cannon and roll of the drums,
    As we go marching on?

Men may die, and moulder in the dust—
Men may die, and arise again from dust,

Hand
in
Hand

62

Shoulder to shoulder, in the ranks of the Just,
　　When Heaven is marching on.

　Glory, glory, hallelujah!
　Glory, glory, hallelujah!
　Glory, glory, hallelujah!
　　His soul is marching on.

Henry Howard Brownell

The Gettysburg Address
NOVEMBER 19, 1863

Fourscore and seven years ago
our fathers brought forth
on this continent
a new nation,
conceived in liberty,
and dedicated to the proposition
that all men
are created equal.

Now we are engaged
in a great civil war,
testing whether that nation,
or any nation so conceived
and so dedicated,
can long endure.

We are met on a great battlefield
of that war.
We have come to dedicate a portion
of that field as a final resting-place
for those who here gave their lives
that that nation might live.
It is altogether fitting and proper
that we should do this.

But in a larger sense,
we cannot dedicate,
we cannot consecrate,
we cannot hallow
this ground.

The brave men,
living and dead, who struggled here,
have consecrated it far above
our poor power to add or detract.

The world will little note, nor long remember,
what we say here, but it can never forget
what they did here.

It is for us, the living,
rather to be dedicated here
to the unfinished work which they
who fought here have thus far so nobly advanced.

It is rather for us to be here
dedicated to the great task remaining before us—
that from these honored dead we take increased devotion
to that cause for which they gave
the last full measure of devotion;
that we here highly resolve
that these dead shall not
have died in vain;
that this nation,
under God,
shall have a new birth of freedom,
and that government
of the people,
by the people,
for the people,
shall not perish
from the earth.

Abraham Lincoln

The Loneliness of Lincoln

At Mount Rushmore I look up into one
Of those faces born joined to the same neck bone.
I said, *Abe, Abe, how does it feel to be up there?*—
And that great rock he has for a pupil budged, I swear,
And he looked me in the eye and he said, *Alone.*

X.J. Kennedy

O Captain! My Captain!

O Captain! my Captain! our fearful trip is done,
The ship has weather'd every rack, the prize we sought is won,
The port is near, the bells I hear, the people all exulting,
While follow eyes the steady keel, the vessel grim and daring;
　　But O heart! heart! heart!
　　　O the bleeding drops of red,
　　　　　Where on the deck my Captain lies,
　　　　　　Fallen cold and dead.

O Captain! my Captain! rise up and hear the bells;
Rise up—for you the flag is flung—for you the bugle trills,
For you bouquets and ribbon'd wreaths—for you the shores a-crowding,
For you they call, the swaying mass, their eager faces turning;
　　Here Captain! dear father!
　　　The arm beneath your head!
　　　　　It is some dream that on the deck.
　　　　　　You've fallen cold and dead.

My Captain does not answer, his lips are pale and still,
My father does not feel my arm, he has no pulse nor will,
The ship is anchor'd safe and sound, its voyage closed and done,
From fearful trip the victor ship comes in with object won;
　　Exult O shores, and ring O bells!
　　　But I with mournful tread,
　　　　　Walk the deck my Captain lies,
　　　　　　Fallen cold and dead.

Walt Whitman

Frederick Douglass
1817–1895

Douglass was someone who,
Had he walked with wary foot
And frightened tread,
From very indecision
Might be dead,
Might have lost his soul,
But instead decided to be bold
And capture every street
On which he set his feet,
To route each path
Toward freedom's goal,
To make each highway
Choose *his* compass' choice,
To all the world he cried,
Hear my voice! . . .
Oh, to be a beast, a bird,
Anything but a slave! he said.

Who would be free
Themselves must strike
The first blow, he said.

He died in 1895.
He is not dead.

Langston Hughes

Marching
On

69

Song of Myself

The runaway slave came to my house and stopt outside,
I heard his motions crackling the twigs of the woodpile,
Through the swung half-door of the kitchen I saw him
    limpsy and weak,
And went where he sat on a log and led him in and assured
    him,
And brought water and fill'd a tub for his sweated body and
    bruis'd feet,
And gave him a room that enter'd from my own, and gave
    him some coarse clean clothes,
And remember perfectly well his revolving eyes and his
    awkwardness,
And remember putting plasters on the galls of his neck
    and ankles;
He staid with me a week before he was recuperated and
    pass'd north,
I had him sit next me at table, my fire-lock lean'd in the
    corner.

Walt Whitman

Barbara Frietchie

Up from the meadows rich with corn,
Clear in the cool September morn,

The clustered spires of Frederick stand
Green-walled by the hills of Maryland.

Round about them orchards sweep,
Apple and peach trees fruited deep,

*Marching
On*

71

Fair as the garden of the Lord,
To the eyes of the famished rebel horde,

On that pleasant morn of the early fall
When Lee marched over the mountain-wall;

Over the mountains winding down,
Horse and foot, into Frederick town.

Forty flags with their silver stars,
Forty flags with their crimson bars,

Flapped in the morning wind: the sun
Of noon looked down, and saw not one.

Up rose old Barbara Frietchie then,
Bowed with her fourscore years and ten;

Bravest of all in Frederick town,
She took up the flag the men hauled down;

In her attic window the staff she set,
To show that one heart was loyal yet.

Up the street came the rebel tread,
Stonewall Jackson riding ahead.

Under his slouched hat left and right
He glanced; the old flag met his sight.

"Halt!"—the dust-brown ranks stood fast.
"Fire!"—out blazed the rifle-blast.

It shivered the window, pane and sash;
It rent the banner with seam and gash.

Quick, as it fell, from the broken staff
Dame Barbara snatched the silken scarf.

She leaned far out on the window-sill,
And shook it forth with a royal will.

"Shoot, if you must, this old gray head,
But spare your country's flag," she said.

A shade of sadness, a blush of shame,
Over the face of the leader came;

The nobler nature within him stirred
To life at that woman's deed and word;

"Who touches a hair of yon gray head
Dies like a dog! March on!" he said.

All day long through Frederick street
Sounded the tread of marching feet:

All day long that free flag tost
Over the heads of the rebel host.

Marching
On

73

Ever its torn folds rose and fell
On the loyal winds that loved it well;

And through the hill-gaps sunset light
Shone over it with a warm good-night.

Barbara Frietchie's work is o'er
And the Rebel rides on his raids no more.

Honor to her! and let a tear
Fall, for her sake, on Stonewall's bier.

Over Barbara Frietchie's grave,
Flag of Freedom and Union, wave!

Peace and order and beauty draw
Round thy symbol of light and law;

And ever the stars above look down
On thy stars below in Frederick town!

John Greenleaf Whittier

The Battle Hymn of the Republic

Mine eyes have seen the glory of the coming of the Lord:
He is trampling out the vintage where the grapes of wrath are stored;
He hath loosed the fateful lightning of His terrible swift sword:
    His truth is marching on.

I have seen Him in the watch-fires of a hundred circling camps,
They have builded Him an altar in the evening dews and damps;
I can read His righteous sentence by the dim and flaring lamps:
    His day is marching on.

I have read a fiery gospel writ in burnished rows of steel:
"As ye deal with my contemners, so with you my grace shall deal;
Let the Hero, born of woman, crush the serpent with his heel,
    Since God is marching on."

He has sounded forth the trumpet that shall never call retreat;
He is sifting out the hearts of men before his judgment seat:
Oh, be swift, my soul, to answer Him! Be jubilant, my feet!
    Our God is marching on.

In the beauty of the lilies Christ was born across the sea,
With a glory in His bosom that transfigures you and me:
As He died to make men holy, let us die to make men free,
    While God is marching on.

Julia Ward Howe

*Marching
On*

75

*F*IVE

I HEAR AMERICA SINGING

LATE 1800S

The Statue of Liberty beckoned with her beacon-hand, and people came from everywhere to "the air-bridged harbor that twin cities frame."

America *was* singing "strong melodious songs"—singing for "spacious skies, for amber waves of grain"—singing, moving on, continuing to explore, build, invent.

Two brothers, Orville and Wilbur Wright, pioneers of aviation, would change the course of travel—and history—forever when they made their first flight in a power-driven aircraft, *Flyer I*, on December 17, 1903, at Kill Devil Hills, North Carolina.

The New Colossus

Not like the brazen giant of Greek fame,
With conquering limbs astride from land to land;
Here at our sea-washed, sunset gates shall stand
A mighty woman with a torch, whose flame
Is the imprisoned lightning, and her name
Mother of Exiles. From her beacon-hand
Glows world-wide welcome; her mild eyes command
The air-bridged harbor that twin cities frame.
"Keep, ancient lands, your storied pomp!" cries she
With silent lips. "Give me your tired, your poor,
Your huddled masses yearning to breathe free,
The wretched refuse of your teeming shore.
Send these, the homeless, tempest-tost to me—
I lift my lamp beside the golden door!"

Emma Lazarus

*Commissioned for an inscription on
the base of the Statue of Liberty*

America, the Beautiful

O beautiful for spacious skies,
    For amber waves of grain,
For purple mountain majesties
    Above the fruited plain!
America! America!
    God shed His grace on thee.
And crown thy good with brotherhood
    From sea to shining sea!

O beautiful for pilgrim feet,
    Whose stern, impassioned stress
A thoroughfare for freedom beat
    Across the wilderness!
America! America!
    God mend thine every flaw,
Confirm thy soul in self-control
    Thy liberty in law!

O beautiful for heroes proved
    In liberating strife,
Who more than self their country loved,
    And mercy more than life!
America! America!
    May God thy gold refine,
Till all success be nobleness
    And every grain divine!

O beautiful for patriot dream
    That sees beyond the years
Thine alabaster cities gleam
    Undimmed by human tears!
America! America!
    God shed His grace on thee.
And crown thy good with brotherhood
    From sea to shining sea!

Katherine Lee Bates

I Hear America Singing

I hear America singing, the varied carols I hear,
Those of mechanics, each one singing his as it should be
    blithe and strong,
The carpenter singing his as he measures his plank or beam,
The mason singing his as he makes ready for work, or
    leaves off work,
The boatman singing what belongs to him in his boat, the
    deckhand singing on the steamboat deck,
The shoemaker singing as he sits on his bench, the hatter
    singing as he stands,
The wood-cutter's song, the ploughboy's on his way in the
    morning, or at noon intermission or at sundown,
The delicious singing of the mother, or of the young wife
    at work, or of the girl sewing and washing,
Each singing what belongs to him or her and to none else,
The day what belongs to the day—at night the party of
    young fellows, robust, friendly,
Singing with open mouths their strong melodious songs.

Walt Whitman

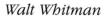

Crazy Boys

Watching buzzards,
Flying kites,
Lazy, crazy boys
The Wrights. They

Tried to fly
Just like a bird
Foolish dreamers
Strange. Absurd. We

Scoffed and scorned
Their dreams of flight
But we were wrong
And they were Wright.

Beverly McLoughland

Flying-Man

Flying-man, Flying-man
Up in the sky,
Where are you going to,
Flying so high?

Over the mountains
And over the sea,
Flying-man, Flying-man
Can't you take me?

Mother Goose

Nat Love: Black Cowboy
1854–1921

Whoever heard of a black cowboy?
You rarely see one in the movies.
You rarely see one on TV.
But I can tell you of *one* black cowboy.
A slave born down in Tennessee.

His name?
        Nat Love.

Occupation:

        cowpuncher
        champion roper
        bronco rider

    (and he's known to have worked cattle from
      the Texas border to Montana).

That Nat Love—
        he was a wanderer
who could handle a rifle
        or a Colt .45
like no other man could.

He could shoot a runnin' buffalo
        at 200 yards.

He was fast.
He had a good eye
He was sharp shootin'
He was double-quick.

    (At one Western-town contest, he earned the name
        DEADWOOD DICK).

You may never've heard of a black cowboy.
You may never've seen one in the movies.
Or on TV.
But now you've heard tell of *one* black cowboy.
Nat Love—
A slave born down in Tennessee.

        Lee Bennett Hopkins

SIX

WHEN JOHNNY COMES MARCHING HOME — AGAIN

EARLY 1900S

From 1914 to 1918 America was engaged in World War I—"the war to end all wars."

But it wasn't.

On December 7, 1941, when Japanese planes struck Pearl Harbor in Hawaii, we were brought into another melee that would shock and shake the entire world.

When Johnny Comes Marching Home, a song first sung during the Civil War, was chanted anew across America as Johnny came marching home—again and again.

Between the wars America witnessed devastating periods of unrest. The Great Depression from 1929 through 1939 took its toll on Americans everywhere.

Bread lines, lack of jobs, despair caused people to wonder if the American dream would ever again be possible.

Unionization became commonplace. Many workers sought protection by joining the fledgling labor movement—the "One Industrial Union Grand."

There Is Power in a Union

Would you have freedom from wage-slavery?
    Then join in the Grand Industrial Band.
Would you from misery and hunger be free?
    Then come do your share like a man.

There is power, there is power
    In a band of working men
        When they stand
        Hand in hand.
That's a power, that's a power
    That must rule in every land,
        One Industrial Union Grand.

Would you have mansions of gold in the sky,
    And live in a shack
    Away in the back?
Would you have wings up in heaven to fly,
    And starve here with rags on your back?

There is power, there is power
    In a band of working men
        When they stand
        Hand in hand.
That's a power, that's a power
    That must rule in every land,
        One Industrial Union Grand.

*When
Johnny
Comes
Marching
Home —
Again*

If you've had enough of the Blood of the Lamb,
    Then join in the Grand Industrial Band.
If, for a change, you would have eggs and ham,
    Then come do your share like a man.

There is power, there is power
    In a band of working men
      When they stand
      Hand in hand.
That's a power, that's a power
    That must rule in every land,
      One Industrial Union Grand.

If you like sluggers to beat off your head,
    Then don't organize,
    All unions despise.
If you want nothing before you are dead,
    Shake hands with your boss and look wise.

There is power, there is power
    In a band of working men
      When they stand
      Hand in hand.
That's a power, that's a power
    That must rule in every land,
      One Industrial Union Grand.

Hand
in
Hand

Come all you workers from every land.
　　Come join the Great Industrial Band.
Then we our share of this earth shall demand.
　　Come on, do your share like a man.

There is power, there is power
　　In a band of working men
　　　　When they stand
　　　　Hand in hand.
That's a power, that's a power
　　That must rule in every land,
　　　　One Industrial Union Grand.

Attributed to Joe Hill

When
Johnny
Comes
Marching
Home —
Again

89

When Johnny Comes Marching Home

When Johnny come marching home again,
Hurrah! hurrah!
We'll give him a hearty welcome then,
Hurrah! hurrah!
The men will cheer, the boys will shout,
The ladies, they will all turn out,
And we'll all feel gay,
When Johnny comes marching home.

The old church-bell will peal with joy,
Hurrah! hurrah!
To welcome home our darling boy,
Hurrah! hurrah!
The village lads and lasses say,
With roses they will strew the way;
And we'll all feel gay,
When Johnny comes marching home.

Get ready for the jubilee,
Hurrah! hurrah!
We'll give the hero three times three,
Hurrah! hurrah!
The laurel-wreath is ready now
To place upon his loyal brow,
And we'll all feel gay,
When Johnny comes marching home.

Let love and friendship on that day,
Hurrah! hurrah!

Their choicest treasures then display,
Hurrah! hurrah!
And let each one perform some part,
To fill with joy the warrior's heart;
And we'll all feel gay,
When Johnny comes marching home.

Patrick Sarsfield Gilmore

The Bean Eaters

They eat beans mostly, this old yellow pair.
Dinner is a casual affair.
Plain chipware on a plain and creaking wood,
Tin flatware.

Two who are Mostly Good.
Two who have lived their day,
But keep on putting on their clothes
And putting things away.

And remembering . . .
Remembering with twinklings and twinges,
As they lean over the beans in their rented back room that
    is full of beads and receipts and dolls and cloths,
    tobacco crumbs, vases and fringes.

Gwendolyn Brooks

*When
Johnny
Comes
Marching
Home —
Again*

What Shall We Do for the Striking Seamen?

What shall we do for the striking seamen?
What shall we do for the striking seamen?
What shall we do for the striking seamen?
    Help them win their battle!

    Oh! Ho! And all together!
    Oh! Ho! And all together!
    Oh! Ho! And all together!
      Help them win their battle!

Turn in food for the striking seamen.
Turn in food for the striking seamen.
Turn in food for the striking seamen.
    Help them win their battle!

    Oh! Ho! And all together!
    Oh! Ho! And all together!
    Oh! Ho! And all together!
      Help them win their battle!

Share our homes with the striking seamen.
Share our homes with the striking seamen.
Share our homes with the striking seamen.
    Help them win their battle!

    Oh! Ho! And all together!
    Oh! Ho! And all together!

Hand
in
Hand

92

Oh! Ho! And all together!
  Help them win their battle!

March on line for the striking seamen!
March on line for the striking seamen!
March on line for the striking seamen!
  Help them win their battle!

Oh! Ho! And all together!
Oh! Ho! And all together!
Oh! Ho! And all together!
  Help them win their battle!

Traditional

Soup

I saw a famous man eating soup.
I say he was lifting a fat broth
Into his mouth with a spoon.
His name was in the newspapers that day
Spelled out in tall black headlines
And thousands of people were talking about him.

  When I saw him,
He sat bending his head over a plate
Putting soup in his mouth with a spoon.

When Johnny Comes Marching Home — Again

Carl Sandburg   93

Madam's Past History

My name is Johnson—
Madam Alberta K.
The Madam stands for business.
I'm smart that way.

I had a
HAIR-DRESSING PARLOR
Before
The depression put
The prices lower.

Then I had a
BARBECUE STAND
Till I got mixed up
With a no-good man.

Cause I had a insurance
The WPA
Said, We can't use you
Wealthy that way.

I said,
DON'T WORRY 'BOUT ME!
Just like the song,
You WPA folks take care of yourself—
And I'll get along.

I do cooking,
Day's work, too!
Alberta K. Johnson
Madam to you.

Langston Hughes

Young Woman at a Window

She sits with
tears on

her cheek
her cheek on

her hand
the child

in her lap
his nose

pressed
to the glass

When
Johnny
Comes
Marching
Home —
Again

William Carlos Williams

FROM

The People, Yes

The little girl saw her first troop parade and asked,
      "What are those?"
"Soldiers."
"What are soldiers?"
"They are for war. They fight and each tries to kill
      as many of the other side as he can."
The girl held still and studied.
"Do you know . . . I know something?"
"Yes, what is it you know?"
"Suppose they'll give a war and nobody will come?"

Carl Sandburg

Hand
in
Hand

96

Depression

We heard people were standing
In bread lines in town.
Everywhere people were begging for work
And nothing much to be found,
That much we knew.
    But we were fine,
    My sister and I,
There on our grandmother's place.

Living in the tenant's house,
Three rooms on a pasture hill,
We had the grass, the trees,
    Fresh air, the sky,
    And all those animals.

We had a father who liked to farm
And a mother who built a bookcase,
Then filled it with books and dreams.

People were begging for work . . .
Were standing in lines for food.
It was a terrible time for many,
But we had everything, my sister and I.
We were growing up rich.

Isabel Joshlin Glaser

*When
Johnny
Comes
Marching
Home —
Again*

97

Mail King

Edward MacDermott
came back from WWII
with one good leg,
and got more mail than anybody
in our building,
and read it
instead of watching TV
which he didn't have—
just two empty TV cabinets
crammed with holiday baking recipes
　　　pet grooming tips
　　　　　seed catalogs
　　　　　　　secrets of oral hygiene
plus maps and brochures
from states coast to coast
and countries we'd never heard of.

One wall was half papered with
　　　a map of China
　　　　　a poster of gold leaves in Vermont
　　　　　　　a stain removal chart.
Mail in his lunch pail.
Sundays and holidays his glum days.

Ruth MacDermott,
with Marilyn Monroe lips but rusty hair,
put up with him—
"I suppose he could have been a drunk,"
she told us once—
until Edward received his mail-order snake
and she put her foot down.
"It's the snake or me."

Edward kept the snake.

Ruth wrote postcards
asking if he still had it.
And Edward did
until by mistake he sucked it up
with his Hoover Deluxe.

When we mailed his apology to Ruth,
he said,
"Thanks, fellas,"
handing Raymond a sample of Tide,
me a catalog of garden supplies.

Paul Janeczko

When
Johnny
Comes
Marching
Home —
Again

101

The Last Good War—and Afterward

We saved enough tinfoil
To wrap the entire world,
Said the Pledge of Allegiance,
Read a chapter of the Bible each day,
And even prayed . . . at school.
Then we turned our radios on,
Went to the movies . . . saw newsreels
    And learned to hate
    Whole nations of people
    We would have to learn
    To love again, later.

Isabel Joshlin Glaser

FROM
Trail Breakers

Pack train, stage coach, pony express, climb over the
    mountain passes;
The Iron Horse roars west, spouting smoke and cinders,
The continental express streaks on, faster, faster, faster.
On the six-lane highways the sleek speedsters are streaming west;
The airliner drones across the sky, six hours from coast to coast.
The jet plane, the supersonic rocket, trail a white line
    across the blue.
The mushroom blast of the H bomb announces
The terror and the splendor of the
Atomic Age.

James Daugherty

*When
Johnny
Comes
Marching
Home —
Again*

103

SEVEN

RIDING TO AND FROM

MID 1900s

After World War II people found themselves on new landscapes—settling in varied areas—riding to and from—on farms, in rural and suburban areas, in the cities.

As they were settling, McCarthyism challenged old traditions, moving America sharply to the right. Senator Joseph McCarthy's committee would silence dissonant views —yet, the American dream was not to be vanquished.

Illinois Farmer

Bury this old Illinois farmer with respect.
He slept the Illinois nights of his life after days of work in Illinois cornfields.
Now he goes on a long sleep.
The wind he listened to in the cornsilk and the tassels, the wind that
    combed his red beard zero mornings when the snow lay white on the
    yellow ears in the bushel basket at the corncrib,
The same wind will now blow over the place here where his hands must
    dream of Illinois corn.

Carl Sandburg

Double Features

Grandma and I used to go
to two double features
each weekend day: sports epics
with Pat O'Brien and Alaska movies
with Michael O'Shea.
And after the movies, the cartoons,
the Pete Smith Specials, and
the newsreels with Hitler's war,
we went to get maple-walnut sundaes
at the local ice cream store.

Ed Rossman

Living in Cheston

FROM *Soda Jerk*

Living in Cheston
is like living in a dream
somebody else is having.
There are days I'm standing
at Maywell's window
and the town freezes up
like stone
for me
and I'm seeing all of us
like it's forever.
Like it's never going to be
any other way
but me being a jerk
and Mr. Jacobs selling paint
and Mr. Brinzer selling chicken legs
and Mrs. Elizabeth Clark
selling little painted bunnies
to hold your messages
to the refrigerator.
There is always
the McCrorys'
and always the Jiff-Lube
and forever the Spin-More records.

I am thinking
there is nothing for God
but Cheston, Virginia,
and no one to create
but us,
and some way we are
knowing everything we have to
and doing
everything we need to
and there's nothing else,
there's nothing more,
but me and this frozen town
that somebody's been dreaming
into life.

Cynthia Rylant

Good Times

my daddy has paid the rent
and the insurance man is gone
and the lights is back on
and my uncle brud has hit
for one dollar straight
and they is good times
good times
good times

my mama has made bread
and grampaw has come
and everybody is drunk
and dancing in the kitchen
and singing in the kitchen
oh these is good times
good times
good times

oh children think about the
good times

Lucille Clifton

Subways Are People

Subways are people—

    People standing
    People sitting
    People swaying to and fro
    Some in suits
    Some in tatters
    People I will never know.

    Some with glasses
    Some without
    Boy with smile
    Girl with frown

    People dashing
    Steel flashing
    Up and down and 'round the town.

Subways are people—

    People old
    People new
    People always on the go
    Racing, running, rushing people
    People I will never know.

Lee Bennett Hopkins

*Riding
to and
From*

109

Commuter

Commuter—one who spends his life
In riding to and from his wife;
A man who shaves and takes a train
And then rides back to shave again.

E.B. White

FROM

Skyscraper

By day the skyscraper looms in the smoke and sun and has a soul.
Prairie and valley, streets of the city, pour people into it and they mingle
    among its twenty floors and are poured out again back to the streets,
    prairies and valleys.
It is the men and women, boys and girls so poured in and out all day
    that give the building a soul of dreams and thoughts and memories.
(Dumped in the sea or fixed in a desert, who would care for the building
    or speak its name or ask a policeman the way to it?)

. . .

Hands of clocks turn to noon hours and each floor empties its men and
    women who go away and eat and come back to work.
Toward the end of the afternoon all work slackens and all jobs go slower
    as the people feel day closing on them.
One by one the floors are emptied. . . . The uniformed elevator men are
    gone. Pails clang. . . . Scrubbers work, talking in foreign tongues.
    Broom and water and mop clean from the floors human dust and
    spit, and machine grime of the day.
Spelled in electric fire on the roof are words telling miles of houses and
    people where to buy a thing for money. The sign speaks till midnight.

. . .

By night the skyscraper looms in the smoke and the stars and has a soul.

Carl Sandburg

Farmer

The farmer, worn from
long, field-days, trods home to a
welcome, warm supper.

Prince Redcloud

Bugs

The lightning bug has wings of gold;
The goldbug wings of flame;
The bedbug has no wings at all,
But it gets there just the same.

Anonymous

Building a New Church

They built the front, upon my word,
    As fine as an abbey;
But thinking they might cheat the Lord,
    They made the back part shabby.

Anonymous

Un-American Investigators

The committee's fat,
Smug, almost secure
Co-religionists
Shiver with delight
In warm manure
As those investigated—
Too brave to name a name—
Have pseudonyms revealed
In Gentile game
    Of who,
    Born Jew,
    Is who?
Is not your name Lipshitz?
    Yes.
Did you not change it
For subversive purposes?
    No.
For nefarious gain?
    Not so.
Are you sure?
The committee shivers
With delight in
Its manure.

Langston Hughes

Riding
to and
From

115

€IGHT

COME WITH DREAMS

LATE 1900s

From the 1960s through the 1990s America witnessed decades of electrifying change—years of peace and love, times of assassinations, riots, unpopular wars, homelessness, fights for a bevy of rights.

"We Shall Overcome" was sung.

Despite the turbulent times there was hope.

Americans have always come with dreams.

The World Is a Beautiful Place

The world is a beautiful place
              to be born into
if you don't mind happiness
              not always being
                          so very much fun
if you don't mind a touch of hell
                  now and then
just when everything is fine
                    because even in heaven
            they don't sing
                    all the time
The world is a beautiful place
                    to be born into
if you don't mind some people dying
                    all the time
or maybe only starving
                    some of the time
            which isn't half so bad
                        if it isn't you.

Lawrence Ferlinghetti

*Come
with
Dreams*

117

Arthur Thinks on Kennedy

When Kennedy
Come to our town
He come with dreams
Got shot right down.

In rained all morning.
You can bet
They didn't want him
Getting wet.

They put a bubble
On his car
So we could see him
From afar.

But then the sun
Come out, so they
Just took the bubble
Clean away.

When Kennedy
Come to our town
Some low-down white folks
Shot him down,

And I got bubbles,
I got dreams,
So I know what
That killing means.

Myra Cohn Livingston

Martin Luther King

Because he took a stand for peace
and dreamed that he would find
a way to spread equality
to all of humankind,

Because he hated violence
and fought with words, not guns,
he won a timely victory
as one of freedom's sons;

Because he died for liberty,
the bells of history ring
to honor the accomplishments
of Martin Luther King.

Aileen Fisher

*Come
with
Dreams*

119

We Shall Overcome

We shall overcome,
We shall overcome,
We shall overcome some day.

Oh, deep in my heart
I know that I do believe
We shall overcome some day.

We shall all be free,
We shall all be free,
We shall all be free some day.

Oh, deep in my heart
I know that I do believe
We shall all be free some day.

We shall walk in peace,
We shall walk in peace,
We shall walk in peace some day.

Oh, deep in my heart
I know that I do believe
We shall walk in peace some day.

We shall brothers be,
We shall brothers be,
We shall brothers be some day.

Hand
in
Hand

120

Oh, deep in my heart
I know that I do believe
We shall brothers be some day.

Truth shall overcome,
Truth shall overcome,
Truth shall overcome some day.

Oh deep in my heart
I know that I do believe
Truth shall overcome some day.

Love shall conquer all,
Love shall conquer all,
Love shall conquer all some day.

Oh, deep in my heart
I know that I do believe
Love shall conquer all some day.

We'll walk hand in hand,
We'll walk hand in hand,
We'll walk hand in hand some day.

Oh, deep in my heart
I know that I do believe
We'll walk hand in hand some day.

Anonymous

Come
with
Dreams

121

en-vi-RON-ment

Homeless People
line up at 8:00 a.m.
sharp
in front of D'Agostino's
on Bethune Street
in Greenwich Village
waiting patiently
for
Automatic Door
to swing open.

They have empty cans.
Sorted.
Placed neatly in rows
in discarded
cardboard flats
or layered in
past-used plastic bags.

A good firm Pepsi is best.
A dented Bud needs
a crack of the fingers
to straighten it back
to its original shape.

A foot-flattened
Orange Crush
is no good to anyone.

Hand
in
Hand

(It gets carefully tossed
into the city-trash-can
on the corner.)

Empty cans are coins.

Coins add up
       to a cup of coffee
       to a bowl of soup
       to a tuna on rye.

Empty cans
are important
to
Homeless People.

They need them
to
feed Them.

And
they help Them
do their conscience-bit
to
protect
the
en-vi-RON-ment.

Lee Bennett Hopkins

*Come
with
Dreams*

125

Vietnam

he was just back
from the war

said the man they got
whites

over there now
fighting
us

and blacks over there
too

fighting us

and we can't tell
our whites
from the others

nor our blacks
from the others

& everybody
is just killing

& killing
like crazy

Clarence Major

We Real Cool

THE POOL PLAYERS.
SEVEN AT THE GOLDEN SHOVEL.

We real cool. We
Left school.   We

Lurk late. We
Strike straight. We

Sing sin. We
Thin gin. We

Jazz June. We
Die soon.

Gwendolyn Brooks

Come
with
Dreams

127

Enemies

We watch
    TV

and see
    enemies fighting.

Close-ups of
      narrow faces
      deep dark eyes
      full young lips.

There are
    two.

Which is an Arab?

    Which is a Jew?

    Charlotte Zolotow

Thought

Of obedience, faith, adhesiveness;
As I stand aloof and look there is to me something
   profoundly affecting in large masses of men following the
   lead of those who do not believe in men.

Walt Whitman

Manhattan Lullaby

(for Richard—one day old)

Now lighted windows climb the dark,
    The streets are dim with snow,
Like tireless beetles, amber-eyed
    The creeping taxis go.
Cars roar through caverns made of steel,
    Shrill sounds the siren horn,
And people dance and die and wed—
    And boys like you are born.

Rachel Field

*Come
with
Dreams*

129

NINE

VOYAGING

1900 AND BEYOND

Voyaging—that is what America is and always has been about—wayfarers, seafarers, airfarers, spacefarers—invention, accomplishments, dreams.

    We march into the present—the future.

    We voyage.

    For liberty of thee we sing.

Midnight Vigil

At twelve o'clock midnight, the lights are cut
 Off. Rushmore's profiles vanish into black.
Still eight wise eyes are never, ever shut,
And never, ever are they looking back.

Then, every tidal basin cherry tree
Is peaceful as that seated man whose stare
Is caring, patient, firm eternally,
Whose eyes are ever wakeful and aware.

Midnight finds her small island silent, yet
The lady with the torch will always keep

Her eyes wide open. She too won't forget
That liberty must never, ever sleep.

Fran Haraway

FROM

A Page of Short Poems

Ending:
    I am tired of the moon, she said,
    Let us go in and turn on the TV.

Voyaging

Eugene J. McCarthy

Post Early for Space

Once we were wayfarers, then seafarers, then airfarers;
We shall be spacefarers soon,
Not voyaging from city to city or from coast to coast,
But from planet to planet and from moon to moon.

This is no fanciful flight of imagination,
No strange, incredible, utterly different thing;
It will come by obstinate thought and calculation
And the old resolve to spread an expanding wing.

We shall see homes established on distant planets,
Friends departing to take up a post on Mars;
They will have perils to meet, but they will meet them,
As the early settlers did on American shores.

We shall buy tickets later, as now we buy them
For a foreign vacation, reserve our seat or berth,
Then spending a holiday month on a moon of Saturn,
Look tenderly back to our little shining Earth.

And those who decide they will not make the journey
Will remember a son up there or a favorite niece,
Eagerly awaiting news from the old home-planet,
And will scribble a line to catch the post for space.

Peter J. Henniker-Heaton

The People, Yes

You can go now yes go now. Go east or west, go north or
    south, you can go now. Or you can go up or go down now.
    And after these there is no place to go. If you say no

    to all of them then you stay here. You don't go. You
    are fixed and put. And from here if you choose you send
    up rockets, you let down buckets. Here then for you
    is the center of things.

Carl Sandburg

U.S.A.

So we march into the present
And it's always rather pleasant
To speculate on what the years ahead of us will see,
For our words and thoughts and attitudes,
All our novelties and platitudes,

Will be Rather Ancient History in 2033.

Voyaging

Rosemary and Stephen Vincent Benét

America

My country, 'tis of thee,
Sweet land of liberty,
Of thee I sing....

Samuel Francis Smith

ACKNOWLEDGMENTS

Every effort has been made to trace the ownership of all copyrighted material and to secure necessary permissions to reprint these selections. In the event of any question arising as to the use of any material, the editor and the publisher, while expressing regret for any inadvertent error, will be happy to make the necessary correction in future printings. Thanks are due to the following for permission to reprint the selections below:

BOA Editions, Ltd. for "Good Times" from *Good Woman: Poems and a Memoir, 1969-1980* by Lucille Clifton. Copyright © 1987 by Lucille Clifton. Reprinted by permission of BOA Editions, Ltd., 92 Park Avenue, Brockport, NY 14420.

Brandt & Brandt Literary Agents, Inc. for "Western Wagons" by Stephen Vincent Benét and Rosemary Carr Benét. From *Selected Works*, Holt, Rinehart & Winston. Copyright 1937, renewed © 1964; excerpt from "U.S.A." by Rosemary Carr Benét and Stephen Vincent Benét. From *A Book of Americans*. Copyright 1933, renewed © 1961 by Rosemary Carr Benét. Reprinted by permission of Brandt & Brandt Literary Agents, Inc.

Gwendolyn Brooks for "We Real Cool" and "The Bean Eaters" from *Blacks*. Copyright 1991, published by Third World Press, Chicago, Illinois, 1991.

The Christian Science Publishing Society for "Post Early for Space" by Peter J. Henniker-Heaton. Reprinted by permission of *The Christian Science Monitor*, copyright 1952 by The Christian Science Publishing Society. All rights reserved.

Curtis Brown, Ltd. for "en-vi-RON-ment" and "John Hancock." Copyright 1994 by Lee Bennett Hopkins. "Nat Love: Black Cowboy: 1854-1921." Originally appeared in *The Crisis*, June-July 1974: Revised edition copyright © 1994 by Lee Bennett Hopkins; "Subways are People" by Lee Bennett Hopkins. Copyright © 1971 by Lee Bennett Hopkins. All reprinted by permission of Curtis Brown, Ltd.

Lillian M. Fisher for "Child of the Sun" and "Pioneers." Used by permission of the author, who controls all rights.

Phil George for "Battle Won Is Lost" from *Native American Arts #1*, published by The Institute of American Indian Arts.

Isabel Joshlin Glaser for "Depression" and "The Last Good War—and Afterward." Used by permission of the author, who controls all rights.

Fran Haraway for "Midnight Vigil." Used by permission of the author, who controls all rights.

Harcourt Brace Jovanovich, Inc. for an excerpt from "A Page of Short Poems" in *Ground Fog and Night* by Eugene J. McCarthy, copyright © 1979 by Eugene J. McCarthy; "Illinois Farmer" from *Cornhuskers* by Carl Sandburg, copyright 1918 by Holt, Rinehart and Winston, Inc., and renewed 1946 by Carl Sandburg; excerpts from *The People, Yes* by Carl Sandburg, copyright 1936 by Harcourt Brace Jovanovich, Inc., and renewed 1964 by Carl Sandburg; excerpt from "Skyscraper" from *Chicago Poems* by Carl Sandburg, copyright 1916 by Holt, Rinehart and Winston, Inc., and renewed 1944 by Carl Sandburg; "Soup" from *Smoke and Steel* by Carl Sandburg, copyright 1920 by Harcourt Brace Jovanovich, Inc., and renewed 1948 by Carl Sandburg. All reprinted by permission of Harcourt Brace Jovanovich, Inc.

HarperCollins Publishers for "Commuter" from *The Lady Is Cold* by E. B. White. Copyright 1925 by E. B. White. Reprinted by permission of HarperCollins Publishers.

Henry Holt and Company, Inc. for "The Gift Outright" from *The Poetry of Robert Frost* edited by Edward Connery Lathem. Copyright 1942 by Robert Frost. Copyright © 1969 by Holt, Rinehart and Winston. Copyright © 1970 by Lesley Frost Ballantine. Reprinted by permission of Henry Holt and Company, Inc.

X. J. Kennedy for "The Loneliness of Lincoln" excerpted from "Edgar's Story," *Cross Ties: Selected Poems* (The University of Georgia Press). Copyright © 1985 by X. J. Kennedy. Reprinted by permission of the author.

Alfred A. Knopf, Inc. for "Madam's Past History" from *Selected Poems* by Langston Hughes. Copyright 1948 by Alfred A. Knopf, Inc.; "Frederick Douglass: 1817-1895" and "Un-American Investigators" from *The Panther and the Lash* by Langston Hughes. Copyright © 1967 by Arna Bontemps and George Houston Bass. All reprinted by permission of Alfred A. Knopf, Inc.

Macmillan Publishing Company for "Manhattan Lullaby" from *Poems* by Rachel Field. Copyright 1936 by Macmillan Publishing Company, renewed 1964 by Arthur S. Pederson. Reprinted by permission of Macmillan Publishing Company.

Beverly McLoughland for "Crazy Boys" and "The Whippoorwill Calls" (originally appeared in *Cobblestone*, February 1981). Used by permission of the author, who controls all rights.

New Directions Publishing Corporation for "The World is a Beautiful Place" from *A Coney Island of the Mind* by Lawrence Ferlinghetti. Copyright © 1958 by Lawrence Ferlinghetti; "Young Woman at a Window" from *The Collected Poems of William Carlos Williams, 1909-1939, volume 1.* Copyright 1938 by New Directions Publishing Corp. Both reprinted by permission of New Directions Publishing Corporation.

The New York Times Company for "Double Features" by Ed Rossman. Copyright © 1992 by The New York Times Company. Reprinted by permission.

Orchard Books for "Mail King" from *Brickyard Summer* by Paul Janeczko. Copyright © 1989 by Paul B. Janeczko; "Living in Cheston" from *Soda Jerk* by Cynthia Rylant. Copyright © 1990 by Cynthia Rylant. Reprinted with permission of the publisher, Orchard Books, New York.

Penguin USA for an excerpt from "Trail Breakers" from *West of Boston* by James Daugherty. Copyright © 1956 by James Daugherty. Renewed © 1985 by Charles Daugherty. Used by permission of Viking Penguin, a division of Penguin Books USA Inc.

Plays, Inc. for "Martin Luther King" from *Year-Round Programs for Young Players*, by Aileen Fisher. Copyright © 1985, 1986 by Aileen Fisher. Reprinted by permission of Plays, Inc., Boston, Massachusetts.

Prince Redcloud for "Farmer." Used by permission of the author, who controls all rights.

Marian Reiner for "Arthur Thinks on Kennedy" from *No Way of Knowing* by Myra Cohn Livingston. Copyright © 1980 by Myra Cohn Livingston; "First Thanksgiving" and "Paul Revere Speaks" from *4-Way Stop and Other Poems* by Myra Cohn Livingston. Copyright © 1976 by Myra Cohn Livingston. Reprinted by permission of Marian Reiner for the author.

Wesleyan University Press for "Vietnam" by Clarence Major from *Swallow the Lake*, copyright 1970 by Clarence Major. Reprinted by permission of Wesleyan University Press by permission of University Press of New England.

Charlotte Zolotow for "Enemies." Copyright © 1990 by Charlotte Zolotow. Used by permission of the author, who controls all rights.

Acknowledgments

INDEX OF TITLES

INDEX OF FIRST LINES

INDEX OF AUTHORS